## About the Bank Street Ready-to-Read Series

More than seventy-five years of educational research, innovative teaching, and quality publishing have earned The Bank Street College of Education its reputation as America's most trusted name in early childhood education.

Because no two children are exactly alike in their development, the Bank Street Ready-to-Read series is written on three levels to accommodate the individual stages of reading readiness of children ages three through eight.

○ *Level 1:* **Getting Ready to Read (Pre-K–Grade 1)**
Level 1 books are perfect for reading aloud with children who are getting ready to read or just starting to read words or phrases. These books feature large type, repetition, and simple sentences.

● *Level 2:* **Reading Together (Grades 1–3)**
These books have slightly smaller type and longer sentences. They are ideal for children beginning to read by themselves who may need help.

○ *Level 3:* **I Can Read It Myself (Grades 2–3)**
These stories are just right for children who can read independently. They offer more complex and challenging stories and sentences.

All three levels of The Bank Street Ready-to-Read books make it easy to select the books most appropriate for your child's development and enable him or her to grow with the series step by step. The levels purposely overlap to reinforce skills and further encourage reading.

We feel that making reading fun is the single most important thing anyone can do to help children become good readers. We hope you will become part of Bank Street's long tradition of learning through sharing.

The Bank Street College of Education

*For J.R.*
*— W.H.H.*

*For Cassandra*
*— R.W.A.*

For a free color catalog describing Gareth Stevens' list of high-quality books and
multimedia programs, call 1-800-542-2595 (USA) or 1-800-461-9120 (Canada).
Gareth Stevens Publishing's Fax: (414) 225-0377.
See our catalog, too, on the World Wide Web: http://gsinc.com

Library of Congress Cataloging-in-Publication Data

Hooks, William H.
    Where's Lulu? / by William H. Hooks; illustrated by R. W. Alley.
        p. cm. -- (Bank Street ready-to-read)
    Summary: Just when Lulu the dog is needed to help play catch with the new
ball from Dad, she cannot be found.
    ISBN 0-8368-1768-0 (lib. bdg.)
    [1. Dogs--Fiction.]   I. Alley, R. W. (Robert W.), ill.   II. Title.   III. Series.
PZ7.H7664Wh   1998
[E]--dc21                                                    97-50492

This edition first published in 1998 by
**Gareth Stevens Publishing**
1555 North RiverCenter Drive, Suite 201
Milwaukee, Wisconsin  53212  USA

Printed in Mexico

1 2 3 4 5 6 7 8 9 02 01 00 99 98

Bank Street Ready-to-Read™

# Where's Lulu?

## by William H. Hooks
## Illustrated by R. W. Alley

A Byron Preiss Book

Gareth Stevens Publishing
**MILWAUKEE**

I found the ball
when I woke up.
It was on the table by my bed.
There was a note on it.
It read:
> For my best pal.
> Love,
> Dad

"Hey, Dad is home," I yelled.
I picked up the ball
and ran down the hall.
"Hey, Dad, this is great!"
I called.
"Can we play catch?"

Mom met me in the hall.
"Shhh," she said.
"Dad is still asleep.
His plane was late."
"Okay," I said.
"Then I'll play with Lulu."

I got dressed
and went downstairs.
"Where's Lulu?" I asked Mom.
"In the kitchen," she said.

I went to the kitchen.
No Lulu.
Only Sam was there,
stuffing his face.
Sam is no fun.
He never wants to play
with me.
"Where's Lulu?" I asked.
"Watching TV," said Sam.

I went into the den.
No Lulu.
Only Sara was there,
watching *Mr. Rogers*.
Sara is too little to play catch.
"Where's Lulu?" I asked.
"She hates *Mr. Rogers*,"
said Sara.
"She went to Bebo's room."

I went to Bebo's room.
No Lulu.
Only Bebo was there,
crunching crackers
all over the floor.
"Where's Lulu?" I asked.
"Da-da-da," said Bebo,
pointing toward the window.
"She went outside?" I asked.
Bebo said, "Da-da-da!"

15

I went outside and called,
"Lulu, where are you?"
No answer.
"Hey, Lulu," I shouted.
"Dad gave me a new ball.
Let's play catch!"
Still no answer from Lulu.

Mrs. Long called to me,
"You shouldn't play
with matches."
She doesn't hear too well.
"No, Mrs. Long," I said.
"I was looking for Lulu
to play *catch*."
"Oh, Lulu," said Mrs. Long.
"I saw her go down
to the cellar."

19

I went down to the cellar.
No Lulu.
Only Grandpa was there,
sawing a board.
"Where's Lulu?" I asked.
"She hates the sound
the saw makes," said Grandpa.
"She left just a minute ago."

I went outside again.
I stood in the yard and yelled,
"Lulu, where are you?"
Still no Lulu.

So I started bouncing the ball
against the fence.
*Thump! Catch!*—
*Thump! Catch!*—

Suddenly, I heard running.
I kept on throwing my ball.
*Thump! Catch!*
*Thump . . .*
*Catch!*

Lulu caught the ball!
Lulu ran around and around
with the ball in her mouth.

I ran after her.
We both got dizzy
and fell on the grass.

Dad came out.
"Can I join you?"
he asked.

So we played three-way catch
all morning.
Can you guess who
never missed a ball?
Lulu!

William H. Hooks is the author of many books for children, including the highly acclaimed *Moss Gown* and, most recently, *The Three Little Pigs and the Fox.* He is also the Director of Publications at Bank Street College. As part of Bank Street's Media Group, he has been closely involved with such projects as the well-known Bank Street Readers and Discoveries: An Individualized Reading Program. Mr. Hooks lives with three cats in a Greenwich Village brownstone in New York City.

R. W. Alley studied at Haverford College and has been illustrating children's books since 1981. He is the author-illustrator of *The Clever Carpenter* and *Watch Out, Cyrus!,* as well as the illustrator of many other children's books including *The Legend of Sleepy Hollow* and *Mrs. Toggle's Zipper.* Mr. Alley lives with his wife and baby daughter in Rhode Island.